UH-OH.

Text copyright © 2020 by Idan Ben-Barak and Julian Frost
Illustrations copyright © 2020 by Julian Frost
Published by Roaring Brook Press
Roaring Brook Press is a division of Holtzbrinck Publishing Holdings Limited Partnership
120 Broadway, New York, NY 10271
mackids.com

Library of Congress Cataloging-in-Publication Data is available.

ISBN 978-1-250-17537-3

Our books may be purchased in bulk for promotional, educational, or business use.
Please contact your local bookseller or the Macmillan Corporate and Premium Sales Department
at (800) 221-7945 ext. 5442 or by email at MacmillanSpecialMarkets@macmillan.com.

First published in Australia in 2020 by Allen & Unwin
First American edition, 2020

Book design by Monique Sterling

Printed in China by Hung Hing Off-set Printing Co., Ltd.
Heshan City Guangdong Province

1 3 5 7 9 10 8 6 4 2

OUCH.

There's a Skeleton Inside You!

IDAN BEN-BARAK and JULIAN FROST

DID THE ENGINE
JUST FALL OFF?

OUCH.

YEP.
OUCH.

I THINK WE MIGHT BE
LATE TO THE PARTY.

ROARING BROOK PRESS

New York

**Quog and Oort are on their way to
Kevin's birthday party.**

Unfortunately, there's been a slight detour.

It looks like they're
going to need a hand.

Turn the page to help Quog and
Oort open the spaceship door.

Give Quog and Oort a wave.

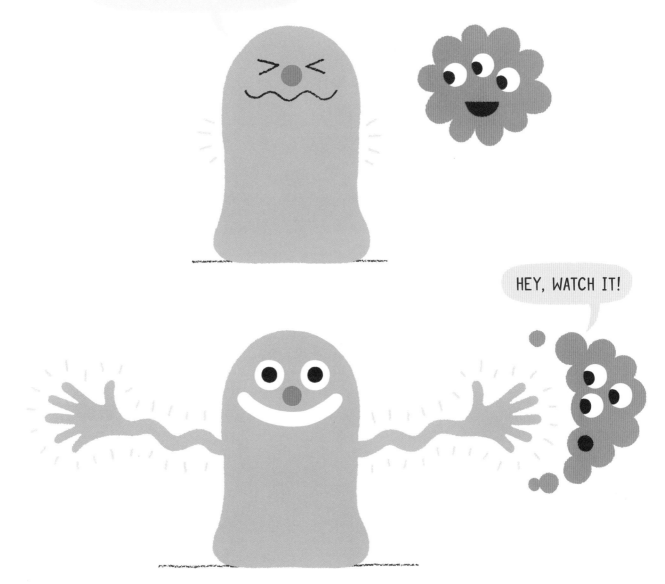

Now it's time for Quog to fix the ship
so they can get to the party.

First, Quog needs to push the engine
down the hill with her new hands.

YOUR HANDS LOOK
KIND OF...FLOPPY.

She seems to be having
some trouble.

Shall we show her how?

**Give the page a push
right here:**

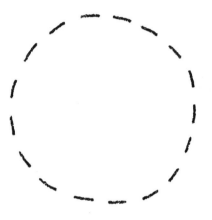

Let's show Quog and Oort what's inside
your hands that keeps them straight.

Place your
right hand here
for a second or two
so Oort can
look inside it.

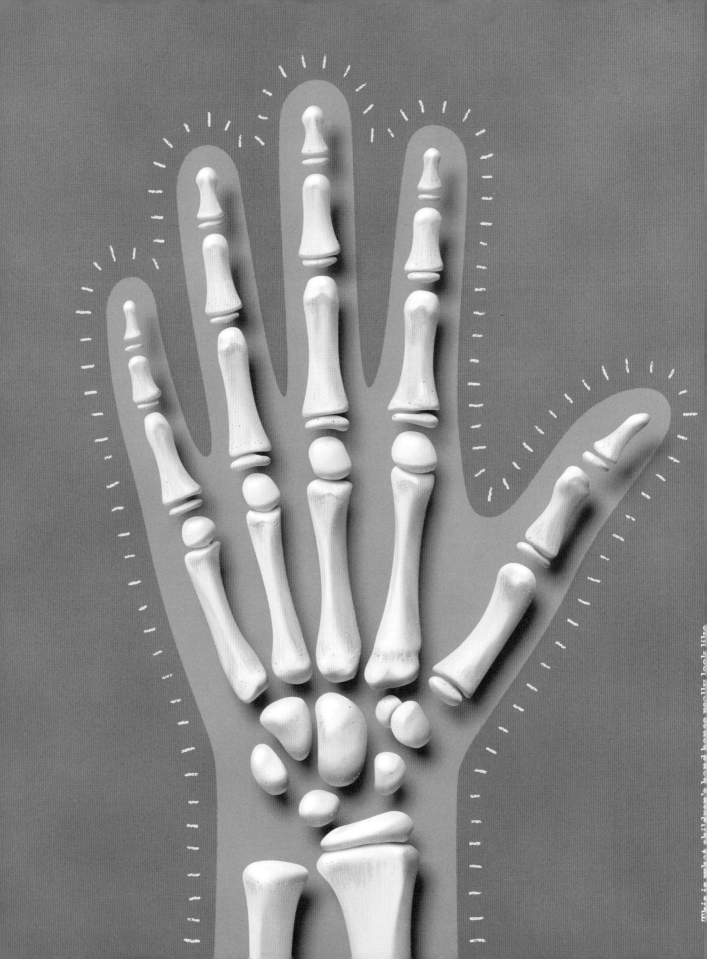

Those are your bones.
They keep your body nice and straight.

Bones give your body structure and help you move.
Without bones you'd be like jelly.

**Now Quog needs to lift the
engine into place.**

NNNNGH!

She seems to be having some trouble.

Shall we show her how?

Lift this book up above your head.

Let's show Quog and Oort what's inside
your hands that makes them strong.

Place your
hand here so Oort
can look inside.

Gently now.

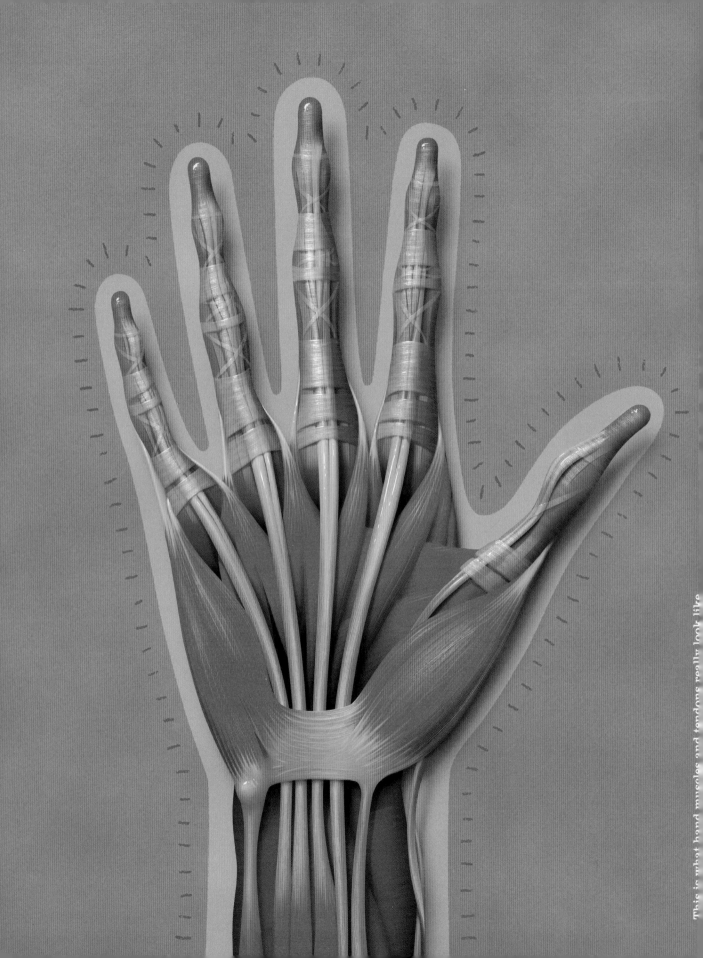

This is what hand muscles and tendons really look like

Those are your muscles.
They give you strength to do stuff.

Muscles connect to your bones. When they
contract they pull the bones and make you move.

The final thing Quog needs to do
is turn the ship's power back on.

Quog seems to be having trouble
feeling with her hands in the dark.

Shall we show her how?

Close your eyes, then turn
the page without looking.

Let's show Quog and Oort what's inside
your hand that lets it feel things.

Place your
hand here so Oort
can look inside.

It might tingle a bit.

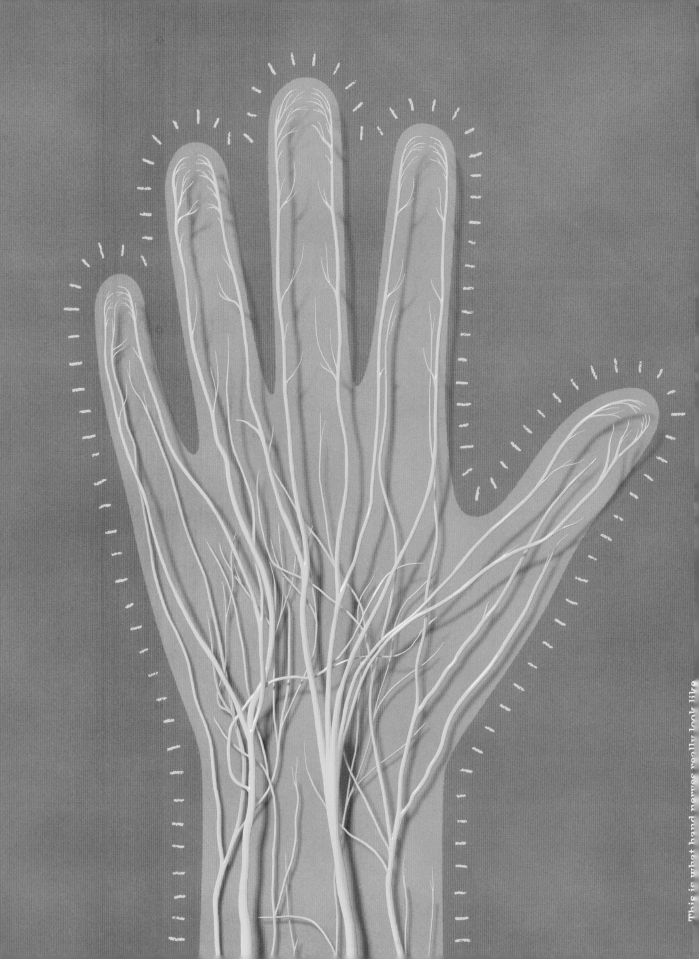

This is what hand nerves really look like

Those are your nerves. They let your hands
feel what you're touching.

Nerves send messages to your brain, telling it about
things like shape, textures, and temperature.

The engine is attached to the spaceship,
the power is on, and Quog and Oort are ready
to blast off to Kevin's birthday party.

Away they go!